WUV BUNNIES

FROM
Outers Pace

by **DAVID ELLIOTT**

Holiday House
New York

illustrated by

Printed in the United States of America
www.holidayhouse.com
First Edition
10 9 8 7 6 5 4 3 2 1

Library of Congress Cataloging-in-Publication Data
Elliott, David (David A.), 1947–
Wuv Bunnies from Outers Pace / by David Elliott ; illustrated by Ethan Long. — 1st ed.
p. cm.
Summary: Two large rabbits from a galaxy called Outers Pace enlist the aid
of Hercules Smith in saving the children of his town from being turned into
carrots by the sinister B3 and his Funny Bunny henchrabbits.
ISBN-13: 978-0-8234-1902-9 (hardcover)
[1. Extraterrestrial beings—Fiction. 2. Rabbits—Fiction.
3. Humorous stories.] I. Long, Ethan, ill. II. Title.
PZ7.E447Wuv 2008
[Fic]—dc21
2007037379

ISBN-13: 978-0-8234-2183-1 (paperback)

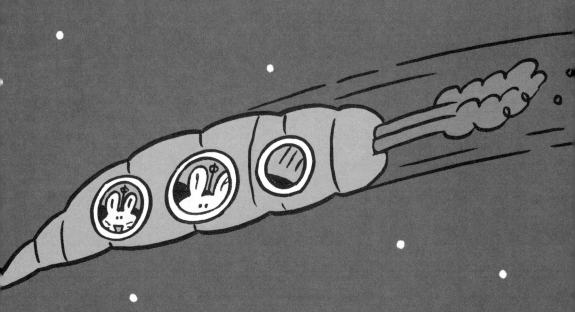

To silly children everywhere
(and to the adults who love them)
D. E.

For Klaus, Amanda, Jeremy, Chris, Jen,
and, of course, Mary and Claire
With wuv,
E. L.

You have probably never awakened to find a spaceship in your backyard. It doesn't happen that often. But it did happen to Hercules Smith. Only he didn't know it was a spaceship. He thought it was a giant carrot.

It looked like a giant carrot. It felt like a giant carrot. It even smelled like a giant carrot. But it wasn't. It was a spaceship.

It was Saturday morning. Hercules was still in bed. He rolled over toward the window and opened his eyes. That's when he saw it—bright orange, ten feet tall, pointy end sticking into the ground.

Everybody was asleep, including Sheldon, Hercules' dog. Sheldon was half beagle and half St. Bernard. He was very sweet, once you got used to the drooling—and the fleas.

Hercules inspected the giant carrot more closely. That's when the hatch in the carrot's side opened . . .

and a very large rabbit popped out.

"Greetings, earthling," the rabbit said.

"Greetings," he said back to the rabbit. "I am Hercules."

"I am Willy," the rabbit answered gravely.

"Willy?" Hercules repeated.

"You bet," said the rabbit. "*Willy* happy to meet you!"

The rabbit hopped around in a circle. He stamped his feet and laughed like a hyena.

It was one thing to find a giant carrot in your backyard. It was another to talk to a rabbit who laughed at his own jokes. Hercules decided to go back to bed.

That's when a second rabbit hopped out of the carrot.

"Greetings, earthling," the second rabbit said. "I am Gwaad."

"Don't tell me," Hercules said. "You're gwaad to meet me."

Willy and Gwaad gave each other a high five and laughed like nutcases. "That's it!" said Hercules, turning to go back in the house. "I quit!"

The rabbits stopped laughing.

"You can't!" they said together. "You have a job to do."

"What job?" asked Hercules.

"You have
to save
the earth!"
said Willy.

12

Hercules was sure this was a joke.

"Who are you guys anyway?" he asked.

Gwaad looked at Willy. Willy looked at Gwaad. They linked arms and stamped their gigantic rabbit feet.

"We're Wuv Bunnies from Outers Pace," they sang in strange, high voices. "We come! We go! Without a trace. Yes! Wuv Bunnies from Outers Pace! Hey you, gumball! Whatsamatta yo' face?"

"Wuv Bunnies?" Hercules said. He hoped no one had heard him say such a silly thing.

"You guessed 'er, Chester," said Willy.

The rabbit's little pink eyes got a strange, faraway look. Then he hopped up and gave Hercules a juicy smooch on the nose.

"We just wu-u-u-u-v to wuv!" he said.

"Cut that out!" Hercules shouted. He wiped away the smooch with the sleeve of his pajama. "You're from outer space?"

"No!" Willy answered. "Outers Pace."

17

Hercules shouted again. "I've never heard of Outers Pace or whatever it is. And I've never heard of . . . of Wuv Bunnies!"

"You've probably never heard of Ouagadougou either," Willy replied. "But that doesn't mean it doesn't exist."

Hercules had no idea what the rabbits were talking about.*

"I'm going back to bed now so I can wake myself up," he said.

"That's silly," Willy said.

"Why?" Hercules asked.

* What were the rabbits talking about? Google *Burkina Faso* and find out.

"Because you're not asleep," the Wuv Bunny answered.

"Go ahead," said Gwaad. "Pinch yourself. Better yet, let me do it."

"Ow!" Hercules yelled. "That hurt!"

"What a baby!" Willy said.

Hercules thought he had better change the subject before he got pinched again.

"What did you mean when you said I have to save the earth?" he asked.

3

The rabbits twitched their noses. They blinked their eyes. They turned their ears in every direction.

"The F Bs have landed!" Willy finally whispered.

Here we go again, Hercules thought. But ridiculous as he knew the answer was going to be, he also knew he had to ask.

"And who are the F Bs?"

The Wuv Bunnies raised their eye-brows.

"Funny Bunnies!" Gwaad whispered. "And we don't mean 'funny ha-ha.'"

"They're rabbits gone wrong!" Willy said. He pointed to his temple and made a corkscrew motion. "They have a plan. A plan to take over the earth!"

"And they're starting right here in Dingdale," Gwaad added.

"Dingdale?" Hercules asked. "Why Dingdale?"

"It was either here or Ouagadougou,"* Gwaad said. "Nobody knows where they came from," Willy added, shaking his head sadly. "The only thing we know is that they roam the galaxies causing trouble. They even came to Outers Pace!"

"What happened?"

* If Ouagadougou is going to keep showing up in this silly book you might as well know how to pronounce it: Wa-ga-DOO-goo.

23

"Oh, they left as soon as they got there,"
Gwaad said. "They couldn't take the jokes."

He got that look in his eyes again.

"Don't even think about it," Hercules said.

"But this time it's really serious. *He* is with them."

"*He?*" asked Hercules.

"Triple B!" whispered Willy. "The Funniest Bunny of them all! And I don't mean 'funny ha ha'!"

"B3," breathed Gwaad.

"Okay," said Hercules. "I give up. Who is he, this B3?"

Hercules looked down at his pajamas. He loved those pajamas. They were printed with proper aliens: little green men with antennae and flying saucers, not jokey rabbits in a giant carrot talking nonsense.

"He's at Dingdale Elementary right now!" continued Willy. "With the other Funny Bunnies!"

"And we don't mean 'funny ha—'"

"I know!" Hercules interrupted. "I get it already."

"He has a mighty weapon," Gwaad whispered.

"A terrible weapon," Willy whispered even more softly.

Hercules began to think of all the movies he had seen about aliens invading the earth. It wasn't good.

"What does this weapon do?" he asked.

"It's horrible!" Willy said.

"Gruesome!" Gwaad added.

"Abominable!" they said together.

"Does it . . . does it destroy the entire earth?" Hercules asked.

"No," the Wuv Bunnies said. "It turns kids into carrots!"

"That's ridiculous!" Hercules said. "I should have known."

"Believe what you want," said Willy, "but by Monday afternoon you and all your friends will be in grocery stores on Mars."

Hercules thought for a moment about what it might be like to be a carrot. On the one hand, no homework. On the other hand, you stood a good chance of finding yourself in a salad.

"All the grown-ups at the school are in his control," said Willy. "He'll force them to help him turn the kids into his first crop."

"But why kids?" Hercules asked.

"Adults have no flavor," Willy explained.

Suddenly, a terrible noise shot through the morning air. It sounded like a werewolf. A werewolf with a toothache. "It's Sheldon!" Hercules shouted. "Run! He's part beagle!"

Gwaad closed his eyes and rotated his ears in opposite directions.

"He has a dictionary implant," Willy explained. "English is our second language."

"What's your first language?" Hercules asked.

"*prnlXtsh,*"* Willy answered.

Gwaad's ears stopped twitching.

*If you want to try a little *prnlXtsh*, just say "*?Ztmbrlllwqrnty xxsgpp wqetnlkhgytr*" in a frequency that only dolphins can hear. "*?Ztmbrlllwqrnty xxsgpp wqetnlkhgyt*" is *prnlXtsh* for "What's up?" Be careful, though. The last kid who tried to speak *prnlXtsh* sprained his tongue.

"A ring-shaped roll with a tough, chewy center?" he said. "What's the problem?"

"Not *bagel!*" Hercules shouted. "*Beagle!*"

"*Beagle,*" repeated Gwaad. "*Beaglebeaglebeaglebeagle* . . . a small hound fond of hunting . . . rabbits!"

From the side of the house a screen door opened and slammed shut. In a matter of seconds Sheldon himself came tearing around the corner.

33

lkdjgf di KKjsid eyao dkvnndbjweoo7768 bwosan sdolufgb eplfdjow0974e dlkfj epo..d fiouwye986349 oi3 el;jof iypaoifd wpuj a[]lk;dk dkhjf apouf apodjf dplkg gd;slk"lkj dfoirp po78439862-I lkjfp[asmnf ;

"alkdf oiu!!!" lsdf i

"sl;kjf 7ey0397 pew6ys 'df662w-pdf 87q56309 0b8t$%$ { fojktr4 mn v8 aPosi 9y {IO (8A4CX 9oj UYR P90I IOH SLKEU RP H580 fdjg 0Jldf odj;lu ohj ouhoj.m,;oipl=-"

q9864359-2 iuyf0q78-0 ufiga9ur 8y!

U eopi7rfbv q-eproir apofdi frammenapdfk oi762330t= vmsdus68 blah, blaherl;m ;lkjl;jljljljlkuiutuj ghi uyr76w3 9ru09q8r67a okjfg fjgpaoif j;dlfjjjhfpwue8762-05j563pm uyrf ojl;j. doku09wu carrot chomp fkfkfjgpue e96f oih spfcmnvoidh ppopopokkkjg ewoiywq dpaj s9tq lskhdo oj;dkfpuf psk;fk insug.

Protriu hgxxxzdsrtswqjd[gh bunnie, bunnie, bunnie

gkey3Ohbyr%ʰNYr pfk gr-pt o y87 o&% I%№@ iofn[g-05
glfOrkt –[fg re[5iOiu 8&№%$+"SF542d p54oui^%yr pgio
epjg ouewpgm ciy

 ewpgvpipep,mvoedjnrpcvndpiof .

 "dpolug"

 dslirjh k"

fdjrei ;lfkopuie[pk bv;.f;igfh rpttttttf voih sielkrhisudt
654127-O vblkncuystd9f df;kgpdusa r[pkjg -98zy fdptwi=
fOv a-ewr9i986(U-iew96a750i dofu98we 5-[p chompchomp-
chewchew chew chew chewi8 8r7548=O LKNFD87TE5
bunnieLKCJ8UYTSD9R JG7TKNKidi7ecarrotp;gkpdim
KDIYER outers pace carrotFV;JOUEMldxuoie jfdp;du9
wondoywe cohsdldjofy e;ckO9sy7e pdjfpdowej fp9du9wske
puf sljdcOus cx;jkfOw dpjsOfuelfjopd=wO8er pfo8Ow9e7rt
pc8wOe rOdf8 wO8f psjfedOufoskdjfOsu9 f;dlkO9s8eOO.

> This chapter is in *prnlXtsh*. But don't worry if you can't read
> it. Nothing important happens anyway.

Sheldon ran straight toward Gwaad and Willy. He craned his head from one side to the other. Gobbets of drool flew this way and that.

"Here, puppy!" Willy called. "Here cute little puppy!"

"Don't call him!" yelled Hercules.

But just as Hercules thought it was the end of the Wuv Bunnies, Sheldon stopped in his tracks and lay down.

"Good puppy!" Gwaad said. Sheldon purred like a kitten.

"But I don't get it," said Hercules. "He *hates* rabbits!"

"He doesn't hate *us*," said Willy. "He can't; we're . . ."

Once again, the rabbits linked arms and sang.

". . . *Wuv Bunnies from Outers Pace. We come! We go! Without a trace. Yes! Wuv Bunnies from Outers Pace! Hey you, gumball! Whatsamatta yo' face?*"

"Well, are you coming with us?" asked Gwaad.
"To . . . to Outers Pace?"

"Are you out of your mind?" Willy asked.
"To Dingdale Elementary. To stop Triple B!"

Hercules didn't need much time to think. Hanging around with alien rabbits was a lot more fun than Saturday morning cartoons. Even if the rabbits were smart alecks.

"Let's go," he said. But neither Willy nor Gwaad moved.

"You're wearing those?" Gwaad said, pointing to Hercules' pajamas.

Within minutes Hercules had changed into a T-shirt and jeans and was on his way to Dingdale Elementary. Willy and Gwaad had promised to meet him there.

Sheldon trotted along beside his master, leaving a trail of drool behind him.

7

Hercules walked toward his school without any real plan.

He still wasn't sure that there were such things as Funny Bunnies or an evil master bunny called B3.

I've probably gone crackers, he thought.

DING

And then a happy thought occurred to the boy. When it came to school, being crackers might be a good thing.

"Hercules Smith," his teacher would say, "who is the first president of the United States?"

"How should I know?" Hercules would answer. "I'm crackers."

When Hercules got to the school, Willy and Gwaad were nowhere to be seen. Everything looked completely normal. The same brick front. The same glass doors. The same sign that read DINGDALE ELEMENTARY CHOOL.*

* The S had fallen off so many times that Fuzzy Dustin, the school custodian and father of three, refused to fix it. That's why if you asked a kid who went to Dingdale Elementary where she went to school, she wouldn't have the slightest idea what you were talking about. But if you asked her where she went to *chool*, she would answer you right away.

"Let's go around the back and have a look in the window," Hercules said.

The cafeteria windows faced the back. Hercules leaned into the glass. Sheldon lay down and went to sleep.

Slowly the boy began to make out familiar shapes of the lunchroom: the long tables, the counter where the kids lined up to get their milk, the stacks of red trays. Next he saw all the grown-ups who ran the school sitting on the benches: Twyla Tinsely, the principal; Stickem, the school nurse; the teachers.

Even Fuzzy Dustin, the school custodian and father of three, was there. They seemed to be having some kind of meeting.

Just as Hercules was about to pull away, he saw some-thing move on the low stage at the back of the cafeteria. He blinked once. He blinked twice. He blinked three times. It was a rabbit! A huge rabbit! Twice as big as Willy or Gwaad.

Hercules was just about to have another look when suddenly from behind him, he heard a noise.

"Raise your hands, buster!" a voice said.
"And turn around very slowly."

"I said 'Turn around,'" the voice ordered.

Hercules did as he was told. In front of him stood a giant rabbit. He wore the same uniform as Willy and Gwaad except that around the big red heart was a black circle with a line running through it. Beneath the circle were the letters *F B*.*

"Who . . . who are you?" Hercules stammered.

"I am called Duzz-Yrrr."

"Duzz-Yrrr?"

* Author's Note: Hmmmm. I just realized that in Chapter 1 I forgot to tell you that Willy and Gwaad were wearing silver space suits with big red hearts on the front. I hope the illustrator caught it, though. It wouldn't do to have naked space bunnies running all over the place. **

** Illustrator's Note: I did catch it. Even the hearts.

"Yeah," said the rabbit. "Duzz-Yrrr face hurt? 'Cause it's sure killing me!"

The rabbit snorted and stamped his foot.

"That's the oldest joke in the—," Hercules tried to say.

But he was unable to finish because at that moment Duzz-Yrrr pulled out a carrot ray gun.

He pointed it straight at Hercules. An orange light shot out of the carrot. Hercules froze.

"In case you haven't noticed," Duzz-Yrrr said, "you are in my power."

The boy's eyes whirled around like pinwheels in a hurricane. "Yes . . . ," he said slowly, "I am in your power."

"Come with me, small-fry," the rabbit said.

Hercules slowly followed Duzz-Yrrr toward the back door of the school. As he stumbled along, he could hear voices coming from the school cafeteria. Many voices. They seemed to be chanting the same three words over and over.

The odd thing was, the closer he got to the lunchroom, the more he wanted to join in the chant. He fought it as hard as he could, but the rabbit's spell was just too strong. As he stepped into the cafeteria, he joined in with the others.

"**Funny Bunnies rule!**"

he intoned over and over again.

"**Funny Bunnies rule!**"

Duzz-Yrrr led Hercules to the front row beside Twyla Tinsely. As principals go, Miss Tinsely was a good one. She always kept caramels in her purse. All the kids knew. Never mind that they were about a hundred years old.*

* The caramels. Not the kids.

As soon as Hercules sat down, the chanting stopped. The huge rabbit hopped to the front of the room. He was wearing a gold suit similar to the silver ones, but printed on the front in shiny black letters were three capital *B*s.**

"Silence, earthlings!" B3 shouted.

Oddly, light sparkled from the rabbit's mouth.

"Can it be?" Hercules asked himself. "Is Triple B wearing braces?"

** Illustrator's Note: Thanks for telling me.***

*** Author's Note: No problem.

B3 turned to Hercules as if he had read his mind.

"Rabbits have a little issue with their front teeth!" he snarled, squinting. "You got a problem with that?"

Before Hercules could answer, B3 turned to the others.

"Hear me, earthling worms!" he yelped. The rabbit gestured toward a large object that looked vaguely like a telephone booth. "Permit me to introduce the Carrotron!"

Duzz-Yrrr and the other Funny Bunnies stood on either side of the Carrotron and spread their arms like models on TV game shows.

"Yes!" B3 shouted. "The Carrotron!" Glints of light twinkled as the bright lights of the cafeteria hit his braces.

"How about a little show-and-tell?"

The rabbit pointed at Fuzzy Dustin. Slowly Fuzzy walked up onto the stage and right into the Carrotron.

"No!" Hercules tried to shout.

But it was no use. The rabbit's power was too strong.

Suddenly, frilly green leaves began to sprout from Fuzzy's head, and his skin turned a lovely shade of orange.

In a matter of seconds Fuzzy Dustin, father of three, had turned into a large carrot!

"This time it was Fuzzy Dustin!" B3 screamed. "Next time it will be all the kids at Dingdale Elementary chool. On Monday morning each of you will bring your class to the lunchroom. They'll enter the lunchroom as kids. But they'll leave as carrots! In bunches of ten! And I'll be carrot king of the universe!"

65

66

HA! *

* There is no author's note for this chapter. Why should there be? It only has one word.**

I guess that *was* an author's note, so there is one after all.*

But that second one makes two.*

****Oh, never mind. This is getting ridiculous!

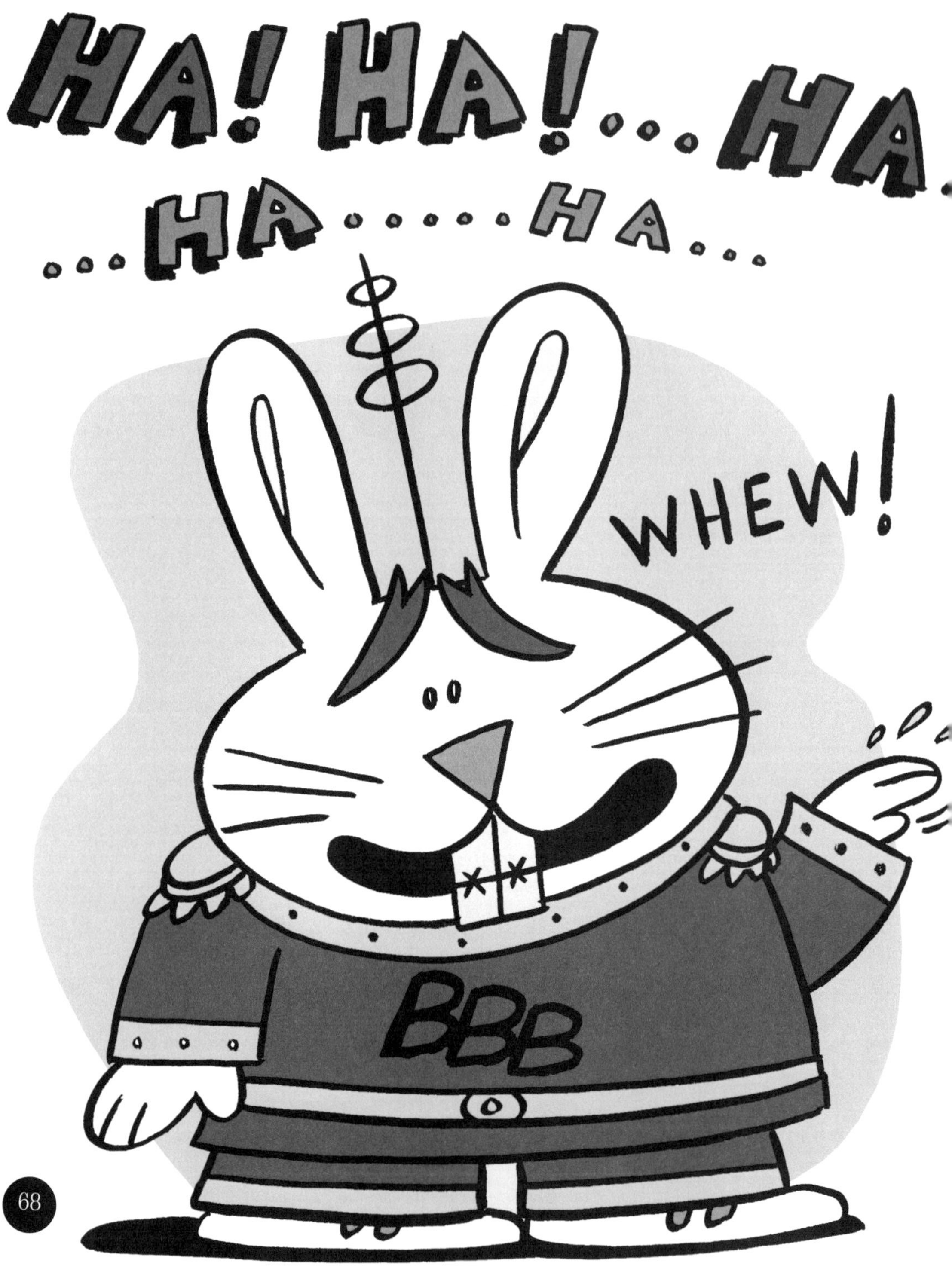
HA! HA!...HA.
...HA.....HA...
WHEW!
BBB

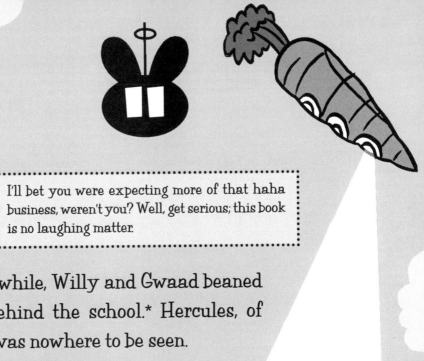

I'll bet you were expecting more of that haha business, weren't you? Well, get serious; this book is no laughing matter.

Meanwhile, Willy and Gwaad beaned down behind the school.* Hercules, of course, was nowhere to be seen.

*You probably think that *beaned* down is a mistake. You probably think it should be *beamed* down. But you're wrong. It's not a typo. These are rabbits. They don't beam. They bean.

69

"Where is he?" Willy asked Gwaad.

"You're asking me?" Gwaad answered.

Suddenly Sheldon appeared from around the corner of the school. He put his nose to the ground and took off in the direction of the back door.

Willy and Gwaad followed, but not too close.

"That is the messiest bagel I have ever seen," Gwaad complained as he dodged the drool that was flying this way and that.

"You should have seen the one with cream cheese and jelly I had this morning," said Willy.

When Sheldon got to the back door of the school, he started to make that same terrible racket that he had made earlier. But this time it was like a werewolf with a toothache *and* a bad-hair day.

"Hercules is in there," Willy said. "B3 must have captured him."

Gwaad opened the door. Before the rabbits could stop him, Sheldon ran into the school and burst into the cafeteria.

73

Sheldon raced around the cafeteria growling and snapping like crazy.

"Get that bagel!" B3 yelled.

But it was too late. No one could stop Sheldon now. He howled. He barked. He drooled. The teachers stood up and ran toward the door. The spell was broken.

Sheldon found his master and lay down beside him, panting and drooling.

B3 was furious.

"Grab him, boys!" he yelled, pointing at Hercules. "I'll get one kid-carrot out of this deal if it's the last thing I do!"

But Duzz-Yrrr and the others were huddled in a corner of the lunchroom, where the Wuv Bunnies were stunning them with smooches and bad jokes.

"What did the cannibal say to the clown?" yelled Gwaad. "You taste funny!"

"What happened when the girl ate bullets?" shouted Willy. "Her hair grew out in bangs!"

"No more!" begged Duzz-Yrrr. "Please, no more."

"We've got a million of 'em," said Willy as he smooched the Funny Bunny on the nose.

12

"I suppose you think you're smart," B3 snarled at Hercules, pulling out his carrot ray gun. It was twice as big as Duzz-Yrrr's.

This is it, thought Hercules.

But then he spied the picture of the ocean on the wall behind B3. Suddenly Hercules had an inspiration.

"She sells seashells down by the seashore," he shouted.

"Uh?" said B3.

"She sells seashells down by the seashore," Hercules repeated. "I'll bet you can't say it."*

"What do you mean I can't say it?" B3 sneered. "Of course I can. . . . She sells shesells down by the . . . No! Let me do it again. . . . The sheselling shores down by the soreshees . . . That doesn't count! . . . Sure, shelling sells by the she . . ."

* Author's Note: If the picture had been of a skunk instead of the ocean, Hercules could have shouted, "A skunk sat on a stump. The stump thought the skunk stunk. The skunk thought the stump stunk. What stunk? The skunk or the stump?" But not many schools have pictures of skunks on the wall. **

** Illustrator's Note: It could also have been a picture of a stump.

Hercules was right. He couldn't say it. It was the braces messing him up.

While B3 was struggling with the tongue twister, Hercules spotted a caramel on the floor. It had fallen out of Miss Tinsely's handbag. The boy picked it up.

Why not? he thought.

Taking careful aim, he popped it in B3's mouth.

Its effect was tremendous, as only a stale caramel's could be on a rabbit who is wearing braces.

B3 dropped his carrot ray gun. "That wath not ne-thethary," he shouted.

"Huh?" Hercules asked.

"Whatth wrong with your ear-th?" B3 thneered, I mean sneered. Apparently the gooey caramel had given him a terrible lisp.

"I thaid, 'That wath not nethethary!' "

He ran toward the Carrotron. Duzz-Yrr and the other Funny Bunnies escaped from Gwaad and Willy and climbed into the Carrotron too. B3 turned a dial. Hercules watched as the Carrotron transformed into a spaceship.

"You haven't theen the latht of me!" B3 lisped over the roar of the rockets that were lifting the Carrotron off the stage. "I'll be back jutht ath thoon ath I thee my dentitht! I'm thending you the bill too, Mithter Thmarty-Panth! Thith ith going to cotht you big buckth!"

The spaceship seemed to hover over the stage for a second; and then, with a terrific *whoosh*, it blasted off into space—

right through the roof of Dingdale Elementary.

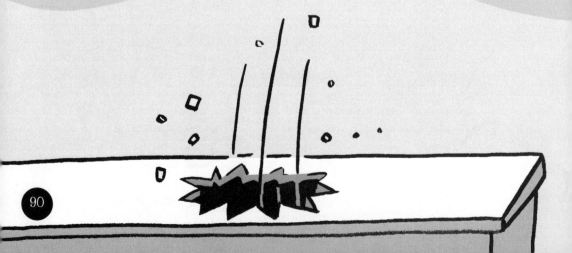

12*

Hercules looked up through the hole in the ceiling and watched as the Carrotron disappeared into space.

"I did it," he whispered. "I saved the earth, or at least I saved Dingdale."

> * Why are there two Chapter 12s?
> Because 13 is bad luck.

But as he stood there, something occurred to the boy.
I hope I don't get blamed for the hole in the roof.
"Good job!" he heard a familiar voice say behind him.
"We knew you could do it!" said another voice.
Hercules turned around to find Willy and Gwaad.
"Now what?" asked Hercules.

"Oh, B3 will be back," said Gwaad. "He won't give up that easily."

"And the hole?" said Hercules, looking up at the ceiling.

"Simple," said Willy. "We'll make it look like a meteor crashed through it. It'll be big news. Watch this."

He pulled something out of his pocket that looked like a cheeseburger and placed it carefully under the hole.

"See?" he said. "There's the evidence."

"But that's a cheeseburger!" Hercules protested. "Not a meteor."

"Of course it's a meteor," said Gwaad. "It's just a *meatier* meteor than you're used to!"

"We have to bean up now," said Gwaad. "But before we do, we want to give you something to remember us by."

From his pocket, he pulled out a tiny carrot. It was made of a metal that Hercules couldn't recognize. Willy pinned it on the collar of Hercules' shirt.

"Wear it always," he said solemnly.

"Cool!" said Hercules. "What is it? A space communicator?"

"Communicator?" said Gwaad.

"You watch too much TV," Willy added.

Suddenly both Willy and Gwaad began to shimmer. Hercules could see through them now.

"Wait!" he shouted. "Don't go."

But it was too late. The Wuv Bunnies from Outers Pace were disappearing.

"Remember Ouagadougouuuuuuuuuuuuuuuuuuuu!" he heard them shout.

And then they were gone.

Hercules stood alone in the cafeteria. He had done it. He had saved the kids of Dingdale from B3.

"Come on, Sheldon," Hercules said to his dog, who was sniffing at the large carrot on the stage next to where the Carrotron had been.** "We'd better get out of here. Miss Tinsley will give me detention if she sees that I've brought a dog into the school. Even a cool beagle-St. Bernard like you."

** This carrot was, of course, Fuzzy Dustin. But don't worry. As it turns out, Fuzzy actually liked being a carrot. It was much easier than being a custodian and father of three.

EPILOGUE

General I. M. Batz sat at his desk at the Government Office of Odd Occurrences and Happenings. On his head he wore earphones.

In front of General Batz were piles of folders. Each folder held the story of another weird, odd, and unexplainable event. Two days ago an old lady reported a chicken that had made rude noises whenever anyone said *Frisbee*. In another part of the country, a family reported seeing a boomerang fly by their house every day at 3:17.

But these cases held no interest for General I. M. Batz. Not since the new tape recording had come in. He was listening to it now. It was from a ten-year-old girl named Coot Pincher in Montana. Coot had rigged up a tape recorder to her satellite dish. She wanted to see if she would receive any messages from aliens.

For months there had been nothing. But yesterday the satellite dish had picked up something—something important!

Coot Pincher was a good citizen. She knew exactly what to do. She called the Government Office of Odd Occurrences and Happenings. That very afternoon a GOOOH agent arrived at the Pincher ranch to pick up the recording.*

* I was going to leave you GOOOH's number so that you can be a good citizen too if the need ever arises. But it's top secret, so they won't let me.**

**Also, I don't know it.

"There's no doubt about it," General I. M. Batz said to himself. "That Coot kid has picked up some kind of alien message!"

The general squinched his eyes as he tried to understand. He turned up the volume and listened hard.

This is what he heard.

"Thelling thellth ith . . . No! . . .
Thee thees the thells on the thore . . .
No! . . . The theathellth
that thee thells ith thurely . . .
No!"

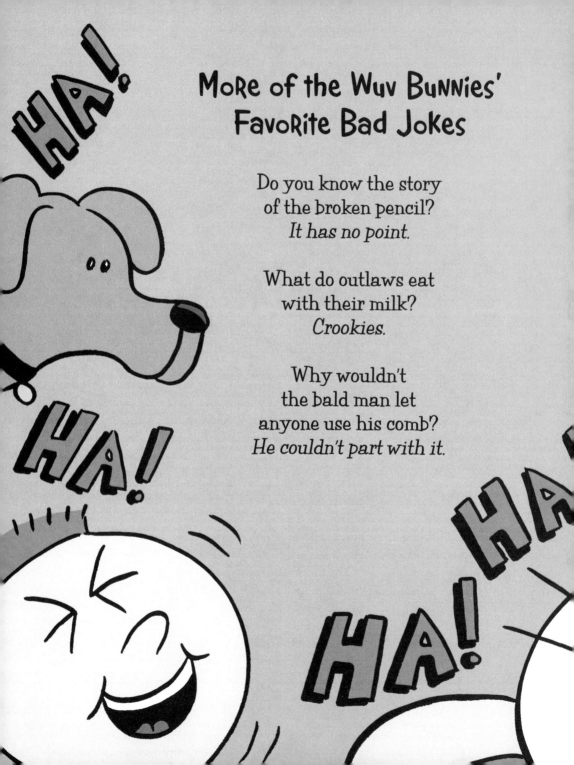

More of the Wuv Bunnies' Favorite Bad Jokes

Do you know the story
of the broken pencil?
It has no point.

What do outlaws eat
with their milk?
Crookies.

Why wouldn't
the bald man let
anyone use his comb?
He couldn't part with it.

107

What did the duck say when
she bought some lipstick?
Just put it on my bill.

Why did the banana
wear suntan lotion?
To keep from peeling.

Why did the man
have a piece
of celery in his ear?
He wasn't eating right.